To Haven !!!

Lelani and

The Plastic Kingdom

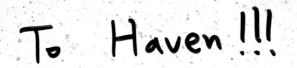

2015

Robb N. Johnston

woohoo!

elani's family lived in a small house, on a small island, in a huge ocean. And today, like almost every other summer day, she was heading down to the beach to spend some time with three of her best friends: sun, sea, and her paddleboard. She waved to classmates from school as she crossed the sand and got into the ocean. She spent the day skimming over the water, laughing and joking, swimming when she felt like it, and lounging on the beach when she needed a break.

It was getting late in the afternoon and just about time to head home when she noticed something floating nearby. A plastic bottle drifting in the water was really nothing special, but something about this one made Lelani scoop it up for closer inspection. She opened it to find a note, written in a bold, flourishing script.

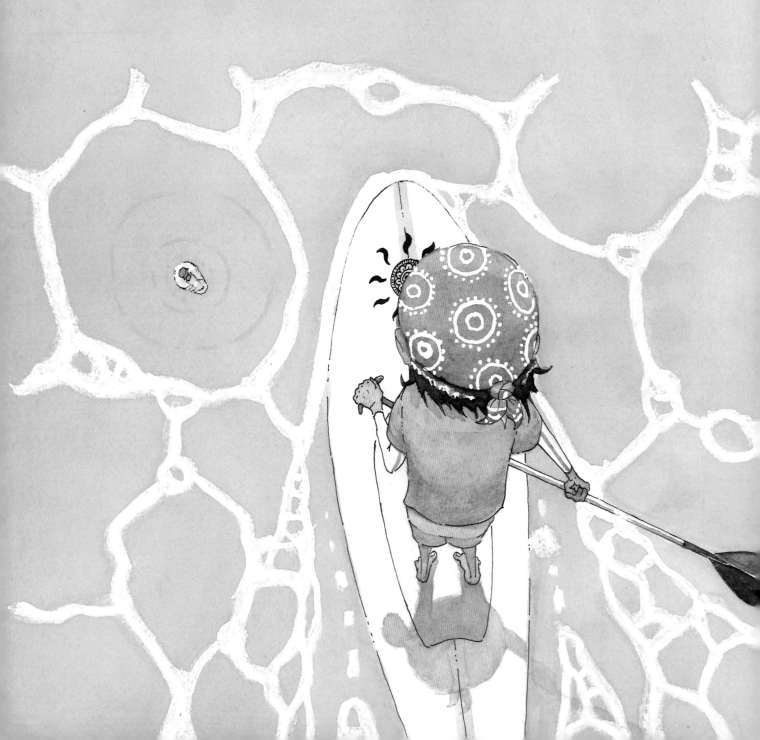

Whosoever holds this note is hereby summoned, with all haste, to the floating kingdom of

New Flotsam.

There, you will attend the court of

His Majesty, The Emperor,

as

"Ambassador to the Fast Lands"

That night, Lelani took the letter out and read it again, just to prove to herself that she wasn't going crazy. "Whosoever holds this note is hereby summoned, with all haste, to the floating kingdom of New Flotsam," it began. "There, you will attend the court of His Majesty, the Emperor, as 'Ambassador to the Fast Lands.'" Lelani drifted off to sleep, excited for her new appointment, and wondering what an ambassador should pack for lunch.

Surprisingly, a lunch fit for an ambassador is almost indistinguishable from a lunch fit for a young girl about to go paddleboarding. So Lelani stuffed her things into her backpack along with her commission to serve as ambassador, and left for the beach.

Lelani carried her board to the water's edge with a sense of purpose and started paddling out to sea. Chloe, a girl she knew from school, was already on the water, and waved to her as she passed. "Hey Lelani! You look like you're on a mission," she called out.

"New job," she replied, "I have to get moving."

"Really? Cool." Said Chloe, "I guess I'll catch you later, then."

Lelani gripped her paddle, set her feet, and pushed herself out past the reef at the mouth of the bay.

The sun was high and hot in the sky when she sat down on her board to eat lunch. An ocean sunfish was basking in the warmth not too far from where she'd stopped. "Excuse me," she said around a mouthful of chicken salad sandwich, "but how much farther to New Flotsam?" If the enormous fish understood, it gave no indication.

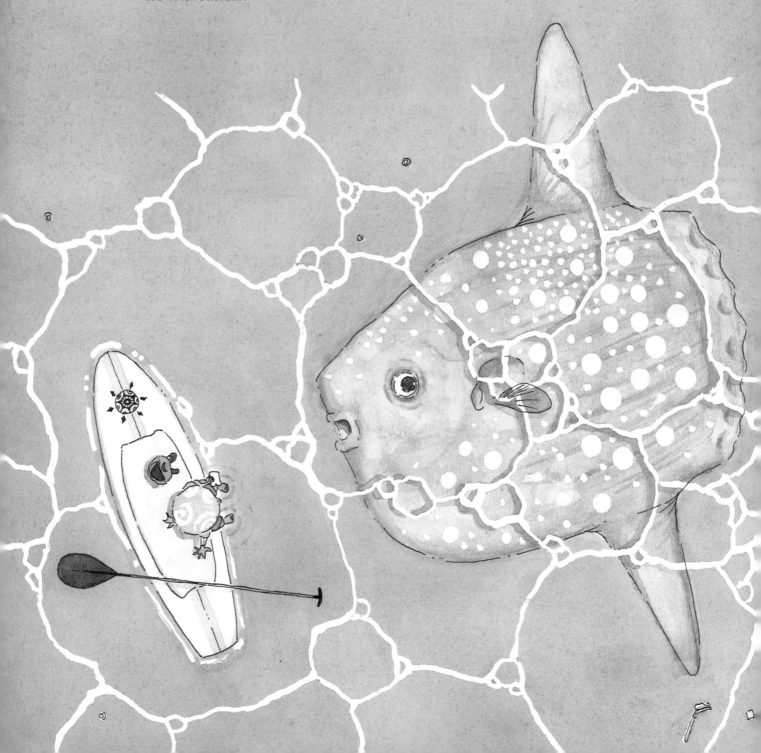

"Well, I guess I'd best be on my way," sighed Lelani,
"Time's a-wasting and those clouds on the horizon look
like trouble."

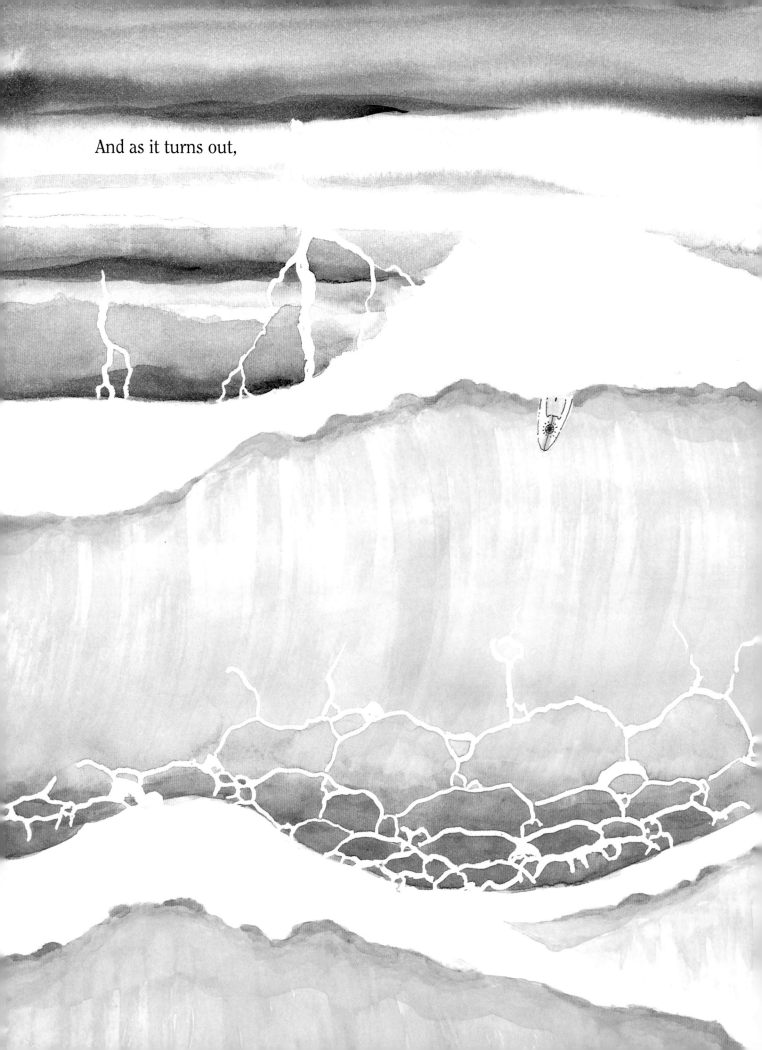

And as it turns out,

they were.

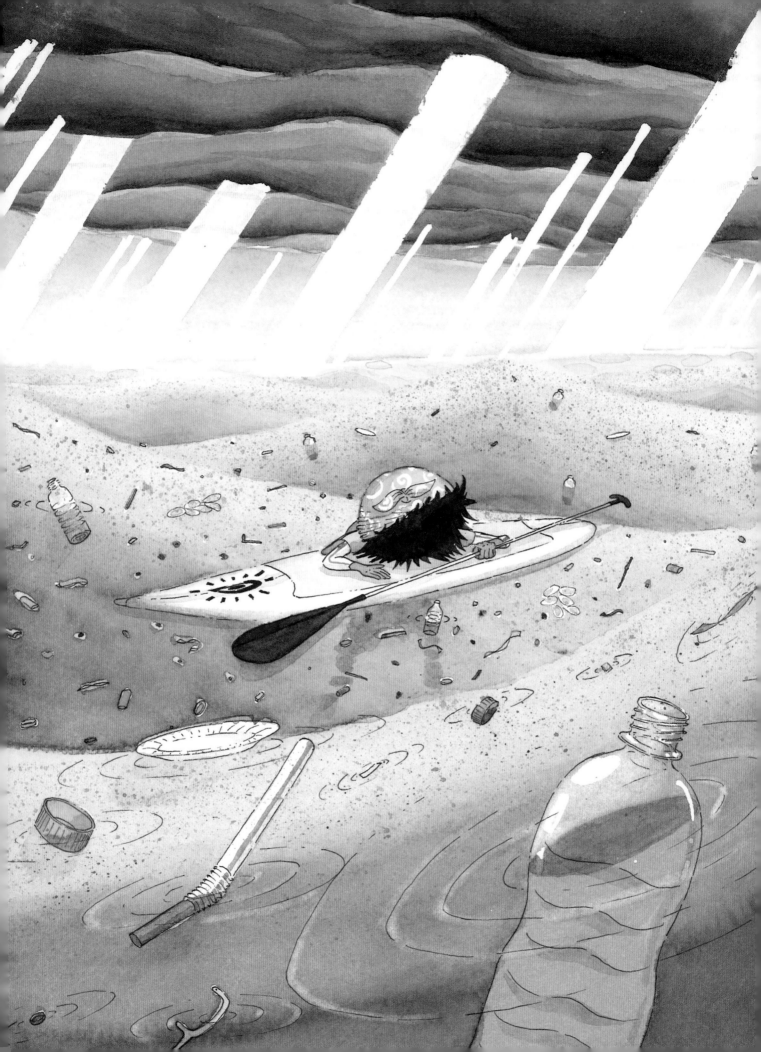

Lelani awoke to the sound of someone politely clearing his throat. Still a little groggy from her voyage, she sat up and blinked in disbelief at what she saw. Standing over her was a boy no older than she. But the similarities pretty much ended there. He wore billowing robes and a flowing cape fastened about his shoulders, all of which looked to be made of plastic bags. On his head, he wore a wreath that also seemed made of plastic bags, woven and braided together. In one hand, he held a brightly colored scepter made of plastic bottle caps. He offered his other hand to Lelani.

"Ah, you're awake!" exclaimed the boy, beaming down at her.

"I guess so…" replied Lelani as she was helped to her feet. "But where exactly am I?" They were clearly on the coast; waves were gently lapping on the peculiar beach. "Is this…?"

"Yes!" he cried, sweeping his arm toward the horizon, "Welcome, Ambassador, to New Flotsam!"

"Reporting for duty, then! …Your Majesty?" Lelani reached into her backpack and presented her commission to the boy.

"Just so!" said the Emperor, handing the paper back and bowing his head graciously.

Lelani smiled, "My name is…"

"No." The Emperor held up his hand to stop her. Lelani was startled. She opened her mouth to speak once more, but the Emperor went on, "I must ask that while you are here, you take a name that fits your office. As my ambassador from New Flotsam to the Fast Lands, you shall be known as Flo." Lelani nodded despite her shock, slowly realizing that a boy she just met had changed her name for her. "As for me," he continued, "it's true that I am the Emperor and ruler of this floating continent, but most of my subjects prefer simply to call me Big Sam. It would please me for you to do the same."

"I can manage that…Sam. I mean, Big Sam."

Big Sam smiled at that, and they started walking away from the coast, toward the interior of the island. They climbed hills and descended into valleys; they saw mountains in the distance across flat, sweeping plains. "I've never seen anything like this place," marveled Flo-but-formerly-Lelani as they walked.

"There is no place like it on Earth," said Big Sam. "My entire kingdom is made of…"

"Plastic," finished Flo.

Big Sam nodded. "Millions and billions of plastic bits. Everything you see is plastic, and there's plastic beneath that as well. An entire island. My island."

"But where does it all come from?" asked Flo.

"The Fast Lands," answered Big Sam. "And that's why you've been summoned here. We'll talk more, but first, we shall get you settled. I'm sure you'll find the Ambassador's Tower to your liking."

"My very own tower," whispered Lelani-except-now-Flo as they made their way across the vastness of New Flotsam.

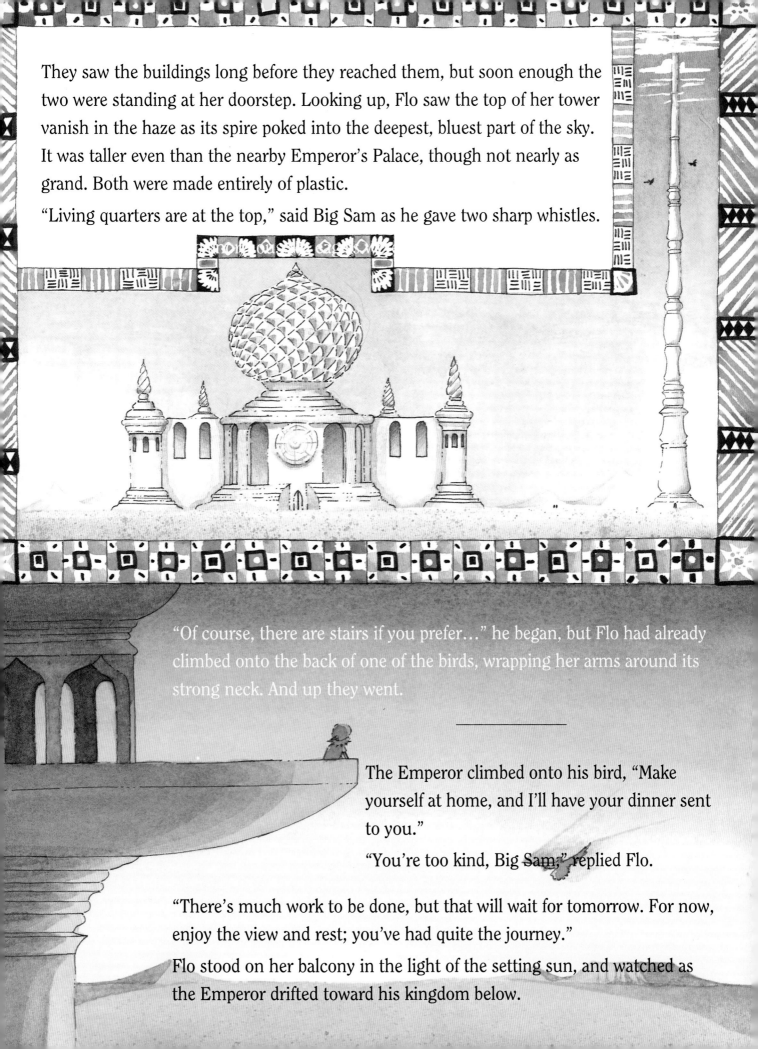

They saw the buildings long before they reached them, but soon enough the two were standing at her doorstep. Looking up, Flo saw the top of her tower vanish in the haze as its spire poked into the deepest, bluest part of the sky. It was taller even than the nearby Emperor's Palace, though not nearly as grand. Both were made entirely of plastic.

"Living quarters are at the top," said Big Sam as he gave two sharp whistles.

"Of course, there are stairs if you prefer…" he began, but Flo had already climbed onto the back of one of the birds, wrapping her arms around its strong neck. And up they went.

The Emperor climbed onto his bird, "Make yourself at home, and I'll have your dinner sent to you."

"You're too kind, Big Sam," replied Flo.

"There's much work to be done, but that will wait for tomorrow. For now, enjoy the view and rest; you've had quite the journey."

Flo stood on her balcony in the light of the setting sun, and watched as the Emperor drifted toward his kingdom below.

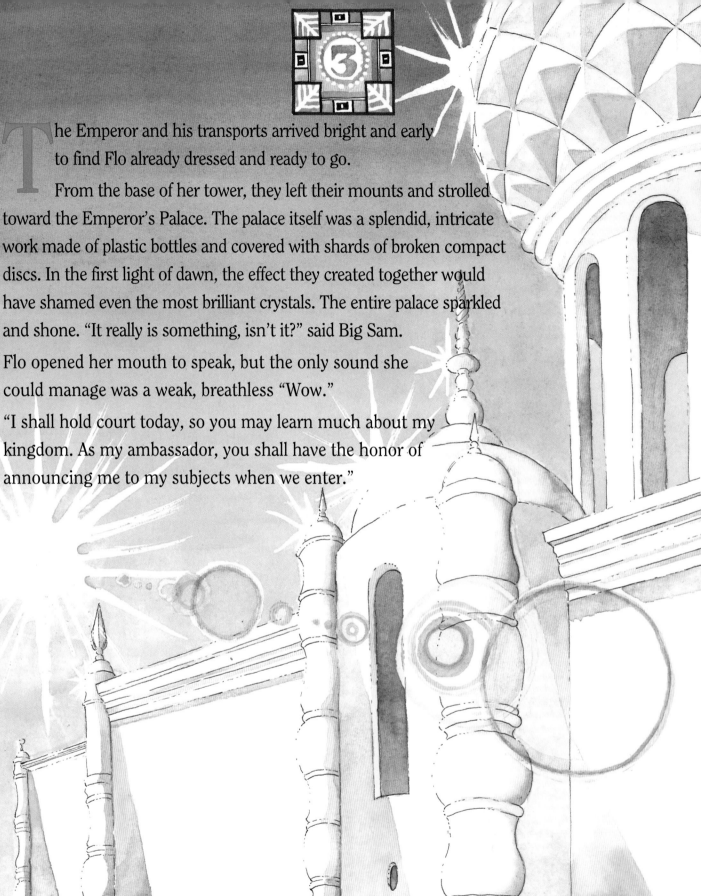

The Emperor and his transports arrived bright and early to find Flo already dressed and ready to go.

From the base of her tower, they left their mounts and strolled toward the Emperor's Palace. The palace itself was a splendid, intricate work made of plastic bottles and covered with shards of broken compact discs. In the first light of dawn, the effect they created together would have shamed even the most brilliant crystals. The entire palace sparkled and shone. "It really is something, isn't it?" said Big Sam.

Flo opened her mouth to speak, but the only sound she could manage was a weak, breathless "Wow."

"I shall hold court today, so you may learn much about my kingdom. As my ambassador, you shall have the honor of announcing me to my subjects when we enter."

Flo nodded and swung the palace doors wide open. She gasped when she saw what was inside.

The hall was cavernous. The ceiling rose higher than any building Flo had ever been inside. Birds of all shapes and sizes soared and whirled in the heights. The floor was just as impressive for its size alone, but was made all the more so by the crowd. Almost every sea creature imaginable was in attendance. Those that weren't standing or waddling around on the floor were milling about in a gigantic pool in the center of the hall.

Flo's eyes could not get big enough to take it all in, so she stood with her mouth open as well. She felt a gentle hand on her shoulder. "Ambassador Flo, if you would be so kind…"

Flo blinked and collected herself. Standing proudly, she cupped her hands around her mouth and announced for the entire hall to hear, "THE SOVEREIGN RULER OF NEW FLOTSAM, HIS MAJESTY THE EMPEROR: BIG SAM."

There was a roar of approval from the crowd as the two made their way to the dais at the back of the hall. Once there, Big Sam raised his hands to quiet the assembly. "I present to you our Ambassador for New Flotsam to the Fast Lands, Flo!" She received a warm welcome, though much less raucous than that for His Majesty. The Emperor's throne was made of the same plastic bits as the island itself, pressed and molded into a handsome seat. Big Sam gestured for Flo to take the smaller chair next to his own. As they sat, Big Sam leaned over and whispered, "Just stay close and see what it means to rule New Flotsam."

Big Sam nodded to the court, and his first subject stepped forward. The sea otter bowed humbly and awkwardly to her ruler. Flo bit her cheek trying to stifle a giggle as the small animal shuffled toward the throne and the Emperor rose to meet her.

He knelt down and gently examined the creature. He titled her head, and exposed the plastic rings of a drink can holder around her neck. "I am sorry for your pain," he told the sea otter, "but I am happy it is so easy to remedy."

He produced a small shark's tooth from his belt, and cut the plastic free. He held it high, and there was cheering from the crowd. The sea otter kissed his hand, and waddled to the edge of the pool, looking back once more before she dove in and disappeared.

The next to come forward was a great sea turtle, ancient and beautiful. Big Sam met him at the edge of the pool as the turtle dipped his beaked head humbly below the surface. The Emperor stroked the turtle's shell and looked him over. The turtle opened its mouth, and the Emperor gave a knowing sigh. "Ah, I see. It is good that you were able to see me before it was too late."

He reached his hand into the turtle's mouth, past the razor-sharp beak, and showed Flo what he pulled out. "A grocery bag?" she asked, "We use those all the time back home."

"Just so," replied Big Sam, "they come to New Flotsam from all corners of the Fast Lands. My subjects often mistake them for jellyfish and try to eat them. Some come to me before they choke…most are not so lucky."

The rest of the day passed in a blur as the menagerie came before the Emperor one by one. Some needed his help or comfort; others came to offer support to the sick and wounded. Flo watched as the Emperor saved a seagull that had been choking on a small plastic toy. She stood by as he soothed and liberated a penguin with its head stuck in a jar. She even stroked a polar bear's muzzle to calm her as Big Sam pulled a sharp plastic sliver from one enormous paw. The Emperor tended to a mackerel, a sailfish, another turtle, and an octopus among others. Some he could help; some he could not. Big Sam gave his full attention to each of his subjects, and received their respect and gratitude in return. For Flo, the most surprising part of what had already been a very unusual day came when the sun was past its peak.

She and the Emperor jumped into the pool in the center of the hall to untangle a sperm whale calf caught in a discarded nylon fishing net. Once free, the whale bowed as delicately as she could, then dove down into the depths below the floating island.

The final petitioner for the day was a pelican, helped forward by three others. Flo knelt beside Big Sam as he inspected the sick bird. "He's very weak," said the Emperor, "he's either eaten too much plastic, or the fish he's been eating have." He whispered something to the bird that Flo could not hear, and the bird lay still in his hands. Silence filled the room. The three remaining pelicans bowed, and took to the sky within the hall.

The Emperor stood, and raised his arms and his voice. "That will conclude our business for the day," he said, "those who seek an audience may come back to court tomorrow."

Creatures that could fly made for the windows in the great hall while others dove into the pool. The rest shuffled to the doorway and spilled out into the evening air.

Big Sam and Flo were the last to leave. The Emperor whistled for an albatross to take Flo to the top of her tower. As the great bird descended toward them, Big Sam put his hand on her shoulder.

"You did very well today. You will make an excellent addition to court."

"I had no idea..." she began, but didn't know what else to say.

"It's been a long, interesting day for you and I'm sure you must be tired," he said. "Go, eat, and rest. We'll talk more tomorrow."

Flo watched the ground and its young ruler fall away as she and her mount climbed higher and higher into the sky.

The next day went much like the first. The Emperor held court and tended to his ailing subjects, great and small. Flo was at his side throughout, helping whenever she was asked, and watching everything. At the end of the day, Flo was waiting for the shuttle to the top of her tower. "So, is it like this every day?" she asked the Emperor.

"Every day," he replied, "And getting worse. There are more and more each day that come to court, seeking my help. And each day there are more I cannot save."

Flo didn't know how to respond to that, so she didn't. As she climbed on the back of the huge bird that would take her up, the Emperor bid her goodnight.

"And one other thing," he added. "Tomorrow I would like you to spend the day exploring my island. I mean for you to be my ambassador to the Fast Lands, so it would be good for you to know the kingdom you represent."

Flo nodded as she stroked the neck of the great bird, "As you wish." She was exhausted but, high in her tower, Flo's last thoughts before sleep came were of exploration and adventure.

The next morning Flo woke to the sound of mighty wings beating the clear morning air. She dressed quickly, looked over the edge of her balcony, and gasped; her tower stood alone over an endless gray expanse. New Flotsam had vanished.

It wasn't until she saw a dull flash far below and heard a distant rumble that she realized what was going on. "A storm," she said out loud. The soaking wet eagle on her balcony dripped in agreement. She climbed on the bird's back and began the descent to the world below. Soon enough, the clear morning sky vanished and Flo was soaring beneath a canopy of gray clouds. Her winged escort flew her away from the palace and the tower, toward the mountains in the distance.

The bird landed on the top of the highest mountain in the range as a gentle rain fell. Flo stepped down onto the peak and wasn't surprised to find it was a mountain made of tiny bits of plastic, most pieces no bigger than grains of sand. She scooped up a handful and let the wet clumps crumble through her fingers. "I'm ready to move on now," she told her chauffer.

Together they flew past waterfalls and out over plains and shifting areas that didn't look so solid. There were also vast lakes, which Flo understood to be holes in the floating island, revealing the ocean beneath. In these, she glimpsed schools of fish and herds of whales, smacks of jellyfish, and even a pod of orcas. Other types of birds accompanied her on the flight, as well as massive flocks of plastic grocery bags, floating and wheeling under the gray sky. Flo climbed down gorges and wandered into caves, exploring all the places her tour guide took her.

Finally, soaked to the bone and exhausted, Flo asked her escort to take her back to the tower.

When they were near the Emperor's Palace, Big Sam was just stepping out. He was clearly tired, but he managed a bright smile for Flo as she touched down and dismounted.

"How was your day of exploration?" he asked. "So sorry about the weather; I suppose even an emperor must bow to the elements."

"Your kingdom is truly immense," she said. Big Sam nodded, knowing it was not entirely a compliment.

"I'm glad you've gotten a sense for the scope of New Flotsam. Our island is unique, would you agree?"

It was Flo's turn to nod knowingly, "An entire continent made of waste from all the other continents."

"You must be eager to dry off and rest. Please join me in court tomorrow," said Big Sam. "I'm sure the weather is beautiful at the top of your tower."

And it was.

Flo spent the next three days attending court with the Emperor and his subjects. She shared in all of their triumphs, all of their sorrows. After court was dismissed, she and Big Sam would explore the kingdom together. They flew to see the vast interior once more, and hiked through an immense forest made completely of drinking straws. They were attended by playful dolphins whilst touring the lakes and rivers that marked the landscape.

On the seventh day, Big Sam was waiting for her at the base of the tower. "Good morning," he said with a smile. "Are you ready to begin your assignment, Ambassador Flo?"

Flo nodded, feelings of purpose, excitement, and sadness swirling together in her heart. "It will be an honor to promote the interests of New Flotsam abroad, Big Sam."

"Then walk with me, and we will see you on your way."

The sun grew higher in the sky, and every now and then Flo would turn to watch the palace and her tower shrink in the distance. Finally, they came to her paddleboard, just as she'd left it on the day of her arrival. Except something was different. "This is wrong. I left my board on the coast, where I washed up. How can it be so far inland?" asked Flo.

"This WAS the coast, a week ago," the Emperor explained. "With each passing day, I become ruler of an ever-larger kingdom." Flo had seen enough in her time on the island to know that Big Sam was not boasting. They picked up her board and paddle and made their way to the coast.

Before long, they were standing together on the edge of Big Sam's domain. They set down Flo's belongings and looked out over the ocean. "Once you leave the island behind you, you may leave the name Flo behind you as well," said the Emperor. "The kingdom of New Flotsam is depending on you to do your duty. Our hope rests with you now."

"But if I succeed in my mission, New Flotsam will be..." began Flo, but she stopped and watched Big Sam.

"True, New Flotsam is my kingdom," he said as he reached into his flowing robes and pulled out a plastic bottle, "but as you have seen during your stay, it's also my prison." He handed her the bottle, and she saw there was a note inside. She took it out and unrolled it, her heart racing.

Whosoever holds this note is hereby summoned, with all haste, to the floating kingdom of

New Flotsam.

There, you will take the name

Big Sam

and preside over the island and its inhabitants as

Emperor and Sovereign.

The note was written in the bold, flourishing script she had seen once before. Sam recited it from memory, never taking his eyes off the ocean: "Whosoever holds this note is hereby summoned, with all haste, to the floating kingdom of New Flotsam. There, you will take the name Big Sam, and preside over the island kingdom and all its inhabitants as Emperor and Sovereign."

Flo's head was spinning. She looked up from the letter and her eyes met Big Sam's, a sad smile on his lips. "How…but, why? Where did you…" she stammered, but he took her hands in his own and she stopped.

"Every kingdom needs a ruler," he explained, "even a floating kingdom made of tiny bits of plastic." Flo looked at him, dumbstruck. Big Sam smiled, "Let me ask you a question, why did you come to New Flotsam after you found *your* note?"

Flo's eyes were starting to well, "I dunno," she said weakly. "Messages in bottles come from those who need help. I'm the one who found that bottle, and…"

"…and I'm so glad you did," finished the Emperor. "But we still have one final order of business before you embark: you must take the 'Ambassador's Oath.'"

Lelani repeated the oath as Big Sam led her through it:

*"I will be a good ambassador
Helping others along the way
To reduce the plastics in our oceans
Little by little, day by day*

*Decisions made in the Fast Lands
No matter how tiny and small
Can have a big effect in New Flotsam
Which is why I have answered the call."*

He helped her move the paddleboard into the water and watched from the shore as she pushed off. "Safe travels, Ambassador," said Big Sam, waving. Flo-for-a-week-but-now-Lelani-again wiped a tear from her cheek and gave a bow.

"I won't let you down, Big Sam," she said, putting all her strength and determination into her voice. She turned her board and made for the open ocean, and the Fast Lands beyond.

Lelani entered the bay early in the evening, and found Chloe paddling around on her board. "Back so soon?" she asked, "Did the new job not work out?"

"I'm actually on assignment," replied Lelani, smiling. "And I have lots of work to do."

Lelani started at home. She convinced her parents and siblings to start sorting their household recyclables. And she offered to help the neighbors do the same. Next, Lelani made herself a bag to take to market, so she wouldn't have to use the plastics from the shopkeepers. She decorated it and made one for her mom as well. Pretty soon, her mom's friends and other people at the market wanted to have them, too. Lelani asked for a reusable water bottle for her birthday, and gave them as presents to her friends on their birthdays as well.

She wrote school reports about the North Pacific Gyre and ghost nets. She sent letters to newspapers promoting recycling programs and urging people to be aware of how much plastic they were throwing away every day.

Lelani was even interviewed by the local news to talk about her newfound passion to reduce plastic in the oceans, and the harm plastics do to marine life. And as news of her work spread, she was soon being interviewed by people from all corners of the Fast Lands.

Lelani saw small changes taking place as people became aware of the impacts their habits were having on the health of the oceans. Gradually, she started to notice big changes. Through it all, she was always just a girl named Lelani, although she knew in her heart she was an ambassador from a floating kingdom, who had once been given the name Flo. She never mentioned New Flotsam, and never spoke of its ruler. Lelani hoped she was doing well as Ambassador to the Fast Lands. Lying in bed at night, she would sometimes think of the floating kingdom and wonder about its young emperor. Would he know how hard she was working? Was there less suffering and heartbreak in his royal court, day after day? Would Big Sam notice if, one day, his island stopped growing? Would he think of his ambassador if one day, miraculously, his kingdom started to shrink? Lelani would drift off to sleep, dreaming of a palace that shone brighter than diamonds, and a tower that reached above the clouds.

Several years had passed since she had plucked that first bottle out of the water and received her commission, and Lelani was heading to the beach with her paddleboard. Friends new and old greeted her as she made her way down to the water. She paddled out and found Chloe sitting on her board, enjoying the warm morning sunshine. "Uh-oh. You have that same go-get-'em look," she said as Lelani paddled past her. Lelani smiled at her friend, "I'm going to see if I still have a job," she replied.

"Oh?" Said Chloe. "Well, I hope you do."

"I don't. But thanks," said Lelani as she paddled out of the bay, leaving Chloe to puzzle over her response.

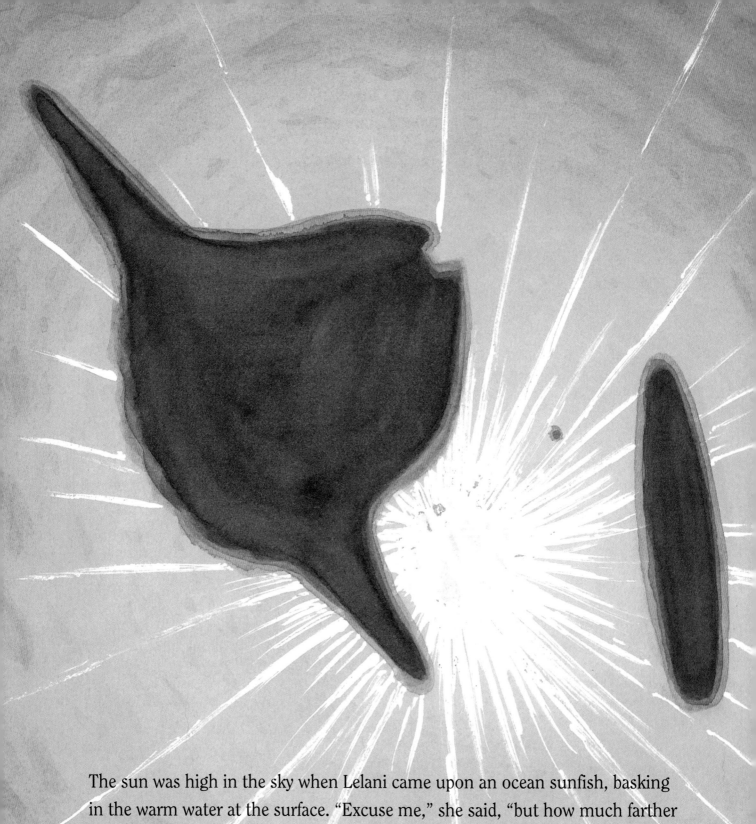

The sun was high in the sky when Lelani came upon an ocean sunfish, basking in the warm water at the surface. "Excuse me," she said, "but how much farther to New Flotsam? I'm the Emperor's Ambassador to the Fast Lands, returning to make my report." If the enormous fish understood, it gave no indication; however, Lelani noticed something bobbing in the water next to it. A plastic bottle floating in the water was a rare sight these days, and everything about this one made Lelani scoop it up for closer inspection. She took a deep breath before opening it and withdrawing the paper within.

Whosoever holds this note is hereby informed that the floating continent of

New Flotsam

is no more. The Emperor is hereby stripped of his property, name, and title, along with all his officers. All inhabitants must depart immediately.

The note was written in a bold, flourishing script, just as she knew it would be. She whispered the words as she read them, "Whosoever holds this note is hereby informed that the floating continent of New Flotsam is no more. The Emperor is hereby stripped of his property, name and title, along with all his officers. All inhabitants must depart immediately."

Lelani read the note a second time, and a third. She threw her head back and yelled into the sky. It was a scream that contained everything she was feeling: sadness, relief, disappointment, a sense of accomplishment, and also happiness. It was the only way to let it all out of her heart at once.

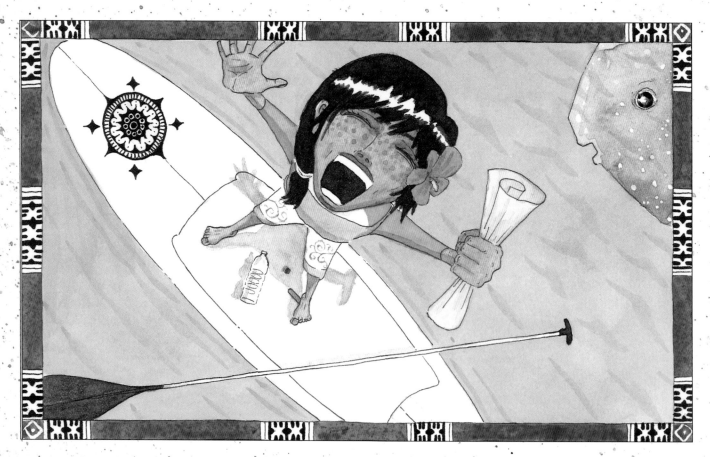

When she'd finished, she stuffed the bottle into her backpack and paddled back the way she'd come.

"Back so soon?" asked Chloe as she slowly paddled by. Lelani smiled and shrugged, and sat on her board next to her friend. "Oh, I see. Sorry about the job." She said, patting Lelani on the shoulder. "Still, I guess it's good you're back. There's a boy on the beach looking for you."

"What? Who?" asked Lelani, startled.

"Nobody has seen him here before," said Chloe. "He's cute."

Lelani stood and paddled to shore. She stepped onto the sand, and saw him walking down the beach. Lelani wasn't sure if she was dreaming, but she let her feet carry her toward him. He was several years taller, and he was wearing swimming trunks instead of his royal plastic robes, but his smile was the same. They were close now, and Lelani could feel her heart beating faster. He hugged her and kissed her on the cheek. "You destroyed my kingdom," he said, his face beaming. "Well done. And thank you." Lelani couldn't stop tears from starting down her cheeks.

"I guess I'm no longer an Ambassador," she said, laughing through her tears. "My name is Lelani."

"And I guess I'm no longer an Emperor," laughed the boy.

"Your name isn't Big Sam, is it?" she asked.

He shook his head, still smiling. He took her hand and they walked down the beach together.

"Will you tell me your name?"

"I will," he said.

And he did.

A note from Robb

New Flotsam exists, but only in our imaginations. You can't actually go there and meet animals from all the corners of the oceans, nor can you explore its towering mountains or its vast, wondrous plains.

But the Great Pacific Garbage Patch DOES exist. It's one of five major gyres to be found in our oceans today, and you CAN go there. What would you see? There would be no tower, certainly no palace; in fact, you would probably not even find a solid place to stand. Instead, you would see a sprawling garbage soup, made of tiny, tiny pieces of plastic, floating in the ocean…stretching from horizon to horizon.

Very few of us will ever visit the gyres, but almost all of us have played some part in filling them with plastic waste. And I believe we can ALL be a part of the solution.

So, what are some things YOU can do to fight plastic pollution in our oceans? One of the biggest changes you can make is to limit single-use plastics in your life, and encourage others to do the same. Plastics in the environment will take THOUSANDS of years to break down, harming marine life all the while…yet we throw away so many plastic items after only one use. Bottles, cups, eating utensils, shopping bags, and straws are just a few examples of the plastic we use, and toss, every day. But these are all things that have durable, sustainable alternatives.

Become an "Ambassador to the Fast Lands!" Educate yourself about the impacts your everyday decisions are having on the world around you, and remember: small changes can make a BIG difference. Just like a small piece of plastic thrown into a tiny river eventually makes its way to the boundless oceans, a positive change you make in your own community echoes out, improving the world in places and times you may never see, for creatures or people you may never meet, in ways that you may never know.